D1368317

This book belongs to:

Sarah

121

Edited by Claire Black
Illustrated by Eric Kincaid

Published by Berryland Books
www.berrylandbooks.com

First published in 2004
Copyright © Berryland Books 2004

ISBN 1-84577-073-0
Printed in China

Goldilocks
and the Three Bears

Reading should always be FUN!

Reading is one of the most important skills your child will learn. It's an exciting challenge that you can enjoy together.

Treasured Tales is a collection of stories that has been carefully written for young readers.

Here are some useful points to help you teach your child to read.

Try to set aside a regular quiet time for reading at least three times a week.

Choose a time of the day when your child is not too tired.

Plan to spend approximately 15 minutes on each session.

Select the book together and spend the first few minutes talking about the title and cover picture.

Spend the next ten minutes listening and encouraging your child to read.

Always allow your child to look at and use the pictures to help them with the story.

Spend the last couple of minutes asking your child about what they have read. You will find a few examples of questions at the bottom of some pages.

Understanding what they have read is as important as the reading itself.

Once upon a time there were three bears who lived in a little house deep inside the woods.

There was Daddy Bear, Mommy Bear and Baby Bear.

Baby Bear was always hungry.

One morning, Mommy Bear made some porridge for breakfast.

Before sitting down to eat, the three bears decided to go for a walk in the woods.

What did Mommy Bear make for breakfast?

by Sarah

Some porridge

A little girl called Goldilocks was also in the woods that day.

She was skipping along when she came across the little house.

Goldilocks was a curious little girl and she wondered who lived there.

She went up to the front door and pushed it open.

"What a beautiful little house!" she said as she went inside.

Goldilocks went into the kitchen and saw the porridge.

"Mmmm! That looks good and I'm feeling very hungry," she said.

She sat down and picked up a spoon.

First she tried Daddy Bear's bowl, but the porridge was too hot.

Then she tried Mommy Bear's bowl, but it was too cold.

Finally, she tried Baby Bear's bowl and it was just right.

"Delicious!" she said and she ate it all up.

After her big breakfast, Goldilocks was feeling very tired and wanted to sit down to rest.

First she tried Daddy Bear's chair, but it was too high.

Then she tried Mommy Bear's chair, but it was too low.

Whose chair will she try next? by sarah

Mommy bear baby bear

Finally, Goldilocks sat down in Baby Bear's chair and it was just right.

Suddenly, the chair broke and Goldilocks fell to the floor!

"Oh no!" she said as she picked herself up.

Goldilocks decided to go upstairs and find somewhere to sleep.

She went into the bedroom and saw three beds in a row.

First she tried Daddy Bear's bed, but it was too hard.

Then she tried Mommy Bear's bed, but it was too soft.

Finally, she tried Baby Bear's bed and it was just right.

She lay down and soon fell asleep.

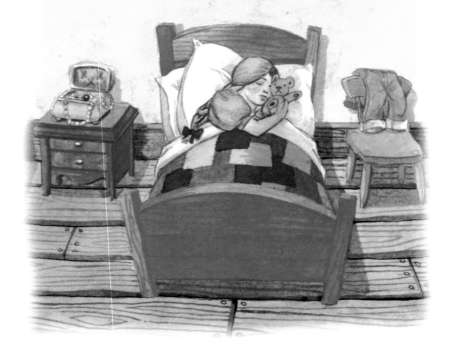

Meanwhile, the three bears were on their way home after their long walk.

Baby Bear was now very hungry.

Saidhs writing

Who are the bears going to find when they get home?

goldi locks

Baby Bear ran into the house and rushed into the kitchen.

He looked inside his bowl and started to cry.

"Oh no! Someone has eaten all my porridge," he cried.

Daddy Bear and Mommy Bear came in and looked into their bowls.

"Someone has been eating our porridge too," Daddy Bear growled.

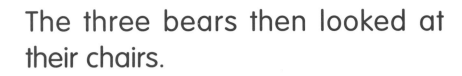

The three bears then looked at their chairs.

"Someone has been sitting in my chair," growled Daddy Bear.

"Someone has been sitting in my chair," growled Mommy Bear.

"Someone has been sitting in my chair and it's broken into pieces!" cried Baby Bear.

Who broke the chair?

Sarahe writ
goldilocks broke it

Daddy Bear looked at Mommy Bear.

"Someone has been in our cottage, eaten our porridge and broken the chair," said Daddy Bear.

"Let's go upstairs and see if anyone is there," said Mommy Bear.

So the three bears crept up the stairs to the top.

Daddy Bear slowly opened the bedroom door and the three bears looked in.

Goldilocks was so tired she had fallen into a deep sleep.

She had not heard the three bears coming home!

She had not heard the three bears climbing the stairs!

The three bears went over and looked at their beds.

"Someone has been sleeping in my bed," said Daddy Bear.

"Someone has been sleeping in my bed," said Mommy Bear.

"Someone is still sleeping in my bed!" said Baby Bear.

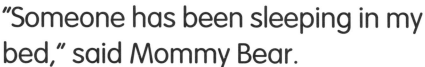

"What?" roared Daddy Bear.

Baby Bear looked at Goldilocks cuddling his teddy bear.

"Wake up!" he shouted.

Goldilocks woke up and saw the three bears beside the bed.

"Who are you?" roared Daddy Bear.

"Who are you?" roared Mommy Bear.

"Who are you and what are you doing in my bed?" squeaked Baby Bear.

Sarahs writing

What do you think Goldilocks will do next?

goldi lock will run away

Goldilocks looked at the bears and said "I'm so sorry!"

Then she jumped out of bed and ran quickly down the stairs and out of the little house.

Goldilocks ran as fast as she could,
all the way home.